A CHRISTMAS PUZZLE

A LADY THEA MYSTERY
BOOK 3.5

JESSICA BAKER

First edition: December 2022.

ISBN: (paperback) 978-1-960102-00-3
ISBN: (e-book) 978-1-960102-01-0

Published 2022 by Jessica Cobine.

ACKNOWLEDGMENTS

Thank you to:
My parents and Audrey
who have always supported and believed in me.

Everyone who has been supportive of me
since I've started this journey.

And all that have read my books.

DISCLAIMER

While it is possible to read this story by itself, for the most enjoyable reading experience, please read Book 1, Murder on the Flying Scotsman, before reading this one.

This story takes place after the events of Book 3, A Most Fashionable Murder.

CHAPTER ONE

Once upon a time, Lady Theodora Prescott-Pryce loved Christmas at Astermore Manor. When she was a child, she used to sneak downstairs into the kitchen with her father and they would drink hot cocoa. She always had been closer to her father than her mother. That was why it hurt so badly when she lost him.

Coming back to the manor now felt like a sore that kept rubbing raw. The good memories she had there had become so tainted by everything else that had happened in the last five years. Her father's wake and funeral. Ilene's introduction to the family and Cecil and Ilene's wedding, where Thea endured endless criticism from her grandmother about how she needed to find a husband before she turned into a spinster. It was something of a blessing that her mother's mother stayed on the other side of the ocean. She claimed this side of the Atlantic didn't agree with her, but Thea privately thought it was because of Aunt Dorothea's death.

Thea's mother got along well with Ilene. She supposed it helped to have a daughter-in-law that you had so many things in common with. It had been strange watching Ilene become like the daughter her mother wanted, despite her mother saying that wasn't actually the case. Ilene's constant judgements about how Thea could improve had destroyed the remains of their friendship beyond repair. Ilene didn't see it that way, but no matter what happened, she didn't think she could ever move past it.

The car slowed in front of the doorway where the staff, along with Cecil and Ilene, had gathered to greet them. Her brother looked painfully bored and Thea wasn't looking forward to being the center of Ilene's mostly undivided attention again.

Why had Wilhelmina and Molly both chosen to stay behind in London? They could have provided some degree of buffer between her and her sister-in-law.

She desperately wished James would join them in the family home, but she also understood why he refused. The relationship between him and their mother was still too new and it wouldn't do to push it too much. Besides, introducing a new family member during the holidays would have sent Cecil into hysterics and she would rather avoid that, especially when she couldn't flee to London.

"You're glowing," she could hear her mother say to Ilene. Thea took a breath and took one of the footmen's hand to step down from the car.

"Thea! Darling, it's so good to see you." Ilene smiled warmly, grasping both of Thea's hands in hers. Her sister-in-law's stomach bulged beneath her dress and one of Thea's hands bumped into it as Ilene let go. It was so strange to think that she would have a new niece or nephew in the new year.

"And you. You look well. Both of you."

Cecil bowed his head. "Welcome home, Mother. Thea."

Why was it so awkward between them? They had grown up beside each other. As a child, she foolishly wished they would become closer as they got older. If Cecil hadn't been the perfect likeness for their father, she might have thought him to be adopted for all that they had in common.

"I'm a bit tired from the journey," Thea said, ignoring the look her mother shot her way. "If you don't mind, I'd like to rest before dinner."

"Of course."

Ilene would never argue with such a request.

It was always strange coming back to Astermore. The house was so familiar, but it didn't feel like home anymore. The furniture had been moved around, the flowers were not the ones her mother used to decorate with, and even the Christmas tree was decorated differently than the tree of her childhood.

Thea walked up the stairs and pretended she was visiting the house of any other extended family member. As a girl, she dreamed about inheriting this house and making changes to suit her tastes. She knew it was impossible. Since she was a daughter, the only way she would ever have gotten this house is if Cecil had died before he married and Thea had married the next heir, a third cousin named Robert Prescott. She never actually considered marrying her cousin on the off chance that her brother might die, but she knew a number of other girls who had, including his wife Cecily.

Her room was unchanged, at least. She didn't know what she would have done if it had been changed, despite having had very little say in how it had been decorated. The dark blue walls were comforting and the mahogany furniture had history. The legend went that the room was used by royalty before Thea was born. In a room like this, she could feel the weight of her legacy pressing down on her shoulders and the expectations others had of her.

In a way, it was strange to sleep among history. She had picked out all new furniture for her room in London when she and her mother moved in there permanently. Her mother felt that a fresh start had been needed and she was correct in that assessment. Thea could still picture her father standing in this room, smiling at her when he presented her with her journal. She missed him more around Christmastime.

"Meow?"

It was a pitiful sound. One of the maids had put Mercury in her room. The poor kitten seemed rather unhappy at the chill in the air, and as a result, he was standing in front of the fireplace looking discontented at the lack of anything for him to climb on or curl into. The bed here was taller than the one at home and the furniture was spaced out enough that he wasn't able to jump. He would need a bed made by the fire so he didn't freeze since she knew he would try to climb off the bed and wake her up in the middle of the night crying when he fell.

For now, though, Thea crouched down and scooped him into her arms, carrying him to the bed. She set him down and pulled off her hat and outer layers. A short nap sounded like a lovely idea.

The door banged open and Bridget's eyes went wide when she saw her. "Beg your pardon, my lady. I didn't realize you'd be up here."

She waved her off. "It's fine."

One of the servants must have brought up her trunk. Before she left, Molly and Wilhelmina had taken great pleasure in packing Thea's wardrobe for the holidays. Blood red gowns with crystal overdresses, emerald green suits, and a variety of other wintery clothes and accessories. She would look like she stepped out of a fashion plate or one of the gorgeous window displays at Fletcher's.

"This place is so different from Prescott House, my lady," Bridget said as she unpacked Thea's trunk into her wardrobe. She must have recognized that Thea didn't seem to be in the best mood and that mindless chatter would be the best way to distract her.

"It is."

"I'll be sharing a room with one of the other maids." She shuffled. "It's odd. I always shared a room at Ravenholm Castle, but I've gotten so used to having my own space at Prescott House that it will be strange sharing again."

She held up one of the gowns and shook it out before hanging it.

Thea took a seat on her bed and immediately, Bridget moved to help her take her boots off. She had quickly learned how to be a proper lady's maid. Despite feeling like a more modern woman, Thea did like having the little conveniences that came with being a lady. Having a proper lady's maid was one of the things she appreciated.

Mercury walked across the bed, plopping his head on her leg. Thea reached down to scratch behind his ears as Bridget took her boots away and went back to unpacking. Thea unbuttoned her blouse. She refused to fall asleep in her corset, and with the way she couldn't stop yawning, sleep would come soon. She stood and Bridget helped her pull her skirt off and unlace her corset before Thea changed into her nightgown.

"Is there anything in particular you'd like to wear to dinner tonight?" Bridget held out one of the dresses, simple, but elegant. "Perhaps this?"

Thea nodded. For the most part, she didn't actually care what she wore while she was here. So long as she looked appropriate, it didn't really matter. She was just counting the days until Christmas and the days until she could go home.

This year, she was particularly glad that she would be able to escape back to London earlier than usual. Her mother normally insisted on them staying until a few weeks before the Season started, but since Wilhelmina and Molly were living in the London house as well, it would be dreadfully rude to leave them alone for so long. As a result, Thea would return just after the new year. She couldn't have been happier.

"Do you think there will be any handsome young men here?"

"I hope not."

Bridget smirked a bit wickedly. "Do you think Inspector Thayne might drop by?"

Thea groaned and pulled Mercury into her lap, despite the kitten's protests. He had grown rather big in the last few months. His fur was shiny and he looked much healthier than he did when she found him.

"I doubt it. His family is in Scotland, so he has no reason to stop by."

She wanted him to though. More than anything.

Thea had spent most of the train ride north pretending to read while fantasizing about Leslie stopping by. The snow would fall gently around them and the tiny flakes would dust his hair and shoulders. There was something incredibly romantic about the idea of him standing in the snow before her. This time, when he leaned in to kiss her cheek to wish her a happy Christmas, she would be bold and she would meet his lips.

He would pull her into his arms then. Her fantasy had taken a wild turn when he asked her to run away with him. Leslie was far too practical to ever actually do so.

"Is there anything else you'd like me to do before I go, my lady? Perhaps draw you a bath?"

Thea shook her head. Her hair would never dry in time for dinner.

"I'll just rest for now."

Bridget smiled and nodded. She closed the lid to the trunk and pushed it back so it wouldn't be in the way before she walked out and closed the door behind her.

Mercury cried out loudly in protest as Thea leaned back. She let him go and he paced helplessly at the edges of the bed.

He let out another wail before jumping to the nightstand, which didn't help him much.

She laughed. "Come here, you silly cat."

She picked him up and set him on the ground. He blinked up at her, his eyes wide. After a few moments, he trotted over to the fireplace and curled on the rug in front of the fire. She envied his ability to be at peace no matter where he was.

———

THEA WOKE FROM HER NAP WITH BRIDGET HOVERING OVER HER in time to change for dinner. The fact that she hadn't heard her maid come in the room bothered her a bit, but she hadn't slept so deeply in months. Thea sat up, blinking the sleep from her eyes.

Bridget helped her get dressed. As she worked, she talked about whatever seemed to come to mind to keep Thea from sinking too deeply into her thoughts. Thea would never go downstairs to dinner if she spent too much time thinking about it.

"Mr. Barton seems nice."

Thea smiled. "He is."

Mr. Barton was the butler at Astermore. He had been there for Thea's whole life. He had started out as a hall boy at the manor when her father was a boy and the two had grown up together. The man had always treated her well, much like a second father.

"Did you find your room all right?"

Bridget nodded. "It's nice. It's so different from Prescott House though. Farley said that if I was a lady's maid for a married lady that I would get my own room." Thea didn't have a clue who exactly Farley was or why Farley would be an authority on lady's maids. Bridget frowned, looking a little bit worried. "Should I have my own room in Prescott House?"

"If Mrs. Green gave you your own room, then I'm sure it's fine."

Mrs. Green, the housekeeper at Prescott House, wouldn't have done something that she knew would offend the others who had lived and worked in the house for ages.

Bridget stuck a pin in Thea's hair. Doing hair was another thing she had improved at. Thea sat still and watched in the mirror. She hoped it was just the four of them tonight. Seeing her grandmother took a bit of mental preparation. Engaging with Prudentia Prescott-Pryce was like preparing for battle, and it was a battle Thea wasn't ready for. It would be bad enough being with Ilene and Cecil.

Tomorrow, she would sneak upstairs to the nursery and see her niece, Zoe. Cecil was far more proper than Father or Mother, so she knew that Zoe probably saw her parents a lot less than Thea had seen hers when she was a child. Right now, Zoe was young enough she wouldn't remember, but she would probably grow up rather lonely, not unlike Thea had.

She climbed down the stairs and walked the familiar route to the drawing room. Music floated out into the hallway from the piano and Thea bit her tongue. She had never been very musically inclined and had tortured the piano in that room more than once as a child. Ilene, on the other hand, always played beautifully. Their teachers used to compliment her in front of the class.

Thea could admit that a part of her had been and still was jealous of Ilene. She found a happiness that felt just out of Thea's reach, no matter how hard she tried.

In school, it had felt like a competition. Ilene wound up being the better hostess, the better musician, the better... well, everything. She had married well, which unless Thea somehow wound up marrying a marquis or a duke, she would hear about it for as long as her grandmother lived. Ilene's father hadn't been an important man, but she had managed to marry one of the few peers in England who wasn't in debt, thanks to the dowries her mother and grandmother brought to their marriages.

Thea peeked into the room between the open doors. The drawing room was empty except for Ilene.

"My lady?" Thea turned, raising a hand to her lips. Mr. Barton lowered his voice. "My lady, is there something I can do for you?"

She shook her head, nodding towards the doors. Understanding passed over his face. She knew what he would have said: a good servant knows exactly what their employer needs. What Thea needed now was not to be left alone with her sister-in-law.

"May I suggest the alcove over there, my lady? You would be much less likely to be spotted."

"Thank you," she whispered.

She tucked herself away behind the wall. Mr. Barton sent her a conspiratorial smile before he continued down to the dining room. All that was left to do was wait.

"…so glad you were able to make it," she heard Cecil saying and Thea went still. It wasn't exactly a hidden secret that she hated most of Cecil's friends, all school boys who had too much privilege and not enough common sense. She knew they weren't schoolboys now, but that didn't make Thea hate them any less.

She caught a flash of dark hair before she pressed herself against the wall. She didn't dare breathe, for fear that they might hear her. Which one of Cecil's friends had dark hair? She couldn't even remember.

A few moments later, she heard the music stop and her mother's footsteps down the stairs and the door to the drawing room opened once more. Thea slipped out from her hiding spot. It was time to join them.

"Thea, you remember my brother Colin," Ilene said with a grin.

Colin Vane had been at the wedding and the numerous other family events since. He was Zoe's godfather, just as Thea was Zoe's godmother. Of all the people that Ilene could have invited, he wasn't the worst.

"Of course I remember him." She smiled at him. They were of the mutual understanding that neither of them was interested in the other.

"He'll be staying with us through the new year. Won't that be lovely?"

Ilene wasn't even subtle about her attempts at manipulating the situation. Ever since she married Cecil, Ilene had tried to convince Colin and Thea that they were perfect for each other. Neither of them felt that way though.

He quirked his lips and lifted his glass to her.

"I'm so sorry to hear that you won't be able to stay as long as usual." Ilene took a bite of food, swallowing and washing it down. "Will you be staying for the servant's ball?"

"Of course. I wouldn't miss it."

Cecil never enjoyed the servant's ball on New Year's day, but Thea always enjoyed it. Mr. Barton always danced with her. When she was younger, she had feelings for one of the footmen. Charley had been a handsome man who had long since moved on to another house that had taken him on as a butler, but before, the ball had been an excuse to see him. To dance with him. And it was socially acceptable for her to do so, only for that one night.

Thea stared down at her plate as they switched out courses. She forced a smile on her face and turned to Mr. Vane.

"I'd love to hear more about what you've been up to in the last few months."

She didn't really, but if it got the focus off of her, she would listen to whatever he had to say.

———

AFTER DINNER, THEA WENT BACK UPSTAIRS. SHE FOUND HER bedroom door cracked open and frowned. She tentatively pushed the door opened and one of the maids, a young girl with a tear-stained soot-smudged face, looked up from by the fireplace. "My lady! I'm so sorry. I didn't realize and the door and—"

"And Mercury escaped."

The girl nodded, choking on sobs. Thea let out a sigh.

"It's not your fault. He would have attempted it sooner or later."

It wasn't like it was the first time he had escaped, even while Thea was watching. He was a little troublemaker.

"I thought I could find him and put him back before dinner, but he's disappeared."

Thea shook her head. "He'll show up, usually when he gets hungry or thirsty or hasn't had enough attention. Just please let the others know to keep an eye out for him so he can get returned up here."

She would go look for him in the morning if he hadn't turned up. But it was more than likely that Mercury would be at her door first thing tomorrow, crying noisily to be let back in.

She went inside and closed the door.

CHAPTER TWO

THEA STARTLED AWAKE AS SOMETHING THUDDED AGAINST THE door. The room was still dark. Was someone trying to break in? She didn't have anything too valuable in her room.

"Meow?"

She sighed and felt blindly for her slippers. The fire had gone down enough that the room was dark. The scullery maid must have gotten distracted when Mercury escaped.

Bridget had cleverly left Thea's dressing gown on the chair by the bed, so she wrapped it around her to fight off the chill. Mercury thumped against the door again as if to tell Thea to move faster.

She rolled her eyes. "I'm coming."

She opened the door and found Mercury peering up at her. A tarnished golden key sat at his feet as he preened up at her the way she imagined he might presenting a dead animal. The faded red tassel didn't help that image.

Thea blinked. The key didn't disappear.

She bent down and scooped up both Mercury and the key. He purred happily and chattered at her, clearly excited about his offering. She held the key up to the light.

"Where did you find this?"

She sighed. What was it for? It was a lovely thing, ornate with delicate scrollwork on it. She couldn't remember ever seeing a key like that before, but someone was bound to notice it was missing later.

She closed the door and set Mercury down again, only to be greeted by the darkness and the chill in the air. Tucking the key into the pocket of her dressing gown, Thea felt along the walls until she found the fire iron. She raked the coals, watching with satisfaction as the flames started to flicker again. She should have just rung for someone, but she loathed the idea of waking someone else up at that hour.

Besides, she could tend to her own fire for one night. She had a feeling that the poor maid would feel horrible about it and she didn't want her to get in trouble. Especially not since it was Mercury's fault.

The kitten lounged contently in the middle of the floor instead of the perfectly good bed that Bridget had made for him before she retired for the night. Little troublemaker.

As if he could read her mind, he looked up at her. If he didn't look so innocent and adorable, he wouldn't get away with nearly as much.

With the room a bit brighter and much warmer, Thea pulled off her dressing gown and climbed into the bed. She hoped Mercury wouldn't decide he wanted on the bed after she fell asleep. He would just have to suffer with his own cozy bed by the fire.

———

BREAKFAST AT ASTERMORE MANOR WAS ONE OF THE FEW TIMES Thea felt a bit resentful about not being married. Since her mother and Ilene were both married, despite her mother being widowed, breakfast was always something of a solitary affair

there. Sure her brother was there, but he never made conversation early in the mornings. He preferred his newspaper,
holding it up like a shield between them.

He'd done the same thing as a child, but when she was
younger, their father had still been alive. Breakfast had been
their time, when her father would ask her about her plans for
the day and talk to her about world events and made her feel
like she was an adult, not just a child trying to understand
world events.

Cecil had already taken his spot at the head of the table.
His newspaper was already up as he mindlessly ate a piece of
toast.

Thea glanced at Mr. Barton, who raised an eye but otherwise didn't comment.

"Good morning," Mr. Vane greeted them.

"Good morning."

Thea brought her plate to the table and sat down. A few
minutes later, Mr. Vane sat across from her.

"I was rather surprised to hear you'd be staying here the
whole time," Thea said.

The last time she saw him, he had been working in his
father's law firm. It was surprising that they would allow him to
take the entire month of December off and Thea found that
rather suspicious.

Mr. Vane smiled mysteriously. "It was kind of my sister to
invite me." Kind, yes, but certainly not without motive. "Our
family has been concerned about her in her condition."

"I'm sure you've missed her."

"Her and my adorable niece. Say, where is she?"

Cecil didn't lower the paper. "She's eating breakfast with
her nurse."

Mr. Vane made a face. From what Thea knew, he and Ilene
grew up middle class. While servants were not uncommon,
their parents had taken a more active role in their childhoods

than Cecil and Ilene took in Zoe's. Cecil always took after their grandmother in that children were meant not to be seen until they were adults.

Thea hated the thought. It seemed too cold an approach. Zoe seemed happy enough now, but what about when she grew older? And if the child Ilene was now carrying was a son, she imagined Cecil would pass his attention completely over Zoe until it came time for her to marry.

"Do you have any plans for the day, Lady Thea?"

Thea shook her head. The key Mercury brought her weighed heavily in her pocket and she itched to go find where it came from.

"I was thinking about going riding. Would you care to join me?"

"Thea doesn't ride," Cecil said without looking up.

"Oh." Was it her imagination, or did Mr. Vane seem disappointed? Not that she actually cared. The thought of getting on a horse still scared her too much.

"I hope you'll enjoy your ride though. The view by the lake is rather lovely this time of year."

The dismissal in her voice was clear.

***

THE WALK UPSTAIRS WAS RATHER QUIET. NO ONE BOTHERED her or asked her what she was doing. Back in her room, Thea pulled the key from her pocket again and ran her fingers over it. Something about it was familiar, but she couldn't place where she knew it from. The feeling left her on edge, tense and waiting for something to happen.

"My lady?"

She jumped and hastily shoved the key back in her pocket as she heard Bridget's voice. Her maid watched her with curious eyes.

"Is something wrong?"

Thea let out a breath. "I don't know."

It was just Bridget. She wouldn't tell her secrets to anyone else. Thea could trust her. She pulled the key back out.

"Mercury brought this to me this morning."

Bridget eyed it, then glanced at the kitten lounging lazily on the bed. She had a lot of feeling about the cat, especially after he led her to believe they were being haunted.

"I don't know where it goes to."

Bridget reached for the key and Thea handed it to her. "It doesn't look like it's been used in some time. It's not shiny and it looks too big to belong to a trunk or something small. Perhaps a door or a safe?"

Unfortunately, in a house like this, that didn't actually narrow it down much. There were dozens of rooms that hadn't been opened in years. Some were closed long before her father's death. Some had been closed even longer. Attempting the key in all of them would be rather time-consuming and probably pointless.

"We need a plan," Bridget said. "Should I ask downstairs?"

Thea thought about it for a moment, then nodded. If someone else knew where it came from, it would be worth it.

They both jumped as Mercury let out an ear-piercing howl.

"What's wrong?" Thea asked him, as if he would actually respond. He stared up at her with that pitiful expression before letting out another howl. She laughed as she realized the problem. "Silly thing," she muttered, picking him up and setting him on the floor. Who knew that leaving him on the bed here would be such an effective way to contain him.

Once he was on the floor, he quieted and trodded over to the door. His paws scratched against it and Thea winced at the marks.

"My lady…"

"I know. The door will need to be fixed."

Bridget shook her head. "Perhaps this idea is crazy, but he's the one who found the key. What if we open the door and follow him? He might lead us to wherever he got it."

Thea blinked. "It's worth a try."

What Thea hadn't anticipated was that the second she opened the door, Mercury squirmed around it, his body almost liquid as he bent to squeeze through the minuscule opening. When she opened the door the rest of the way, he was already disappearing around the corner.

She glanced at Bridget before they both chased after him.

"What a little devil," Bridget gasped, as it was clear Mercury had indeed slipped away from them again.

CHAPTER THREE

LESS THAN A WEEK INTO HER STAY AT ASTERMORE CAME THE day Thea had been dreading. As Thea headed down to breakfast, Mr. Barton held a silver tray out to her. A cream-colored envelope with a wax seal laid in the center of the tray and she knew immediately who it was from. She took the letter and the letter opener beside it, sliding it through the paper and listening with a minuscule degree of satisfaction as it ripped open, even as her stomach tangled into a multitude of knots.

> *Theodora,*
> *It has come to my attention that you have arrived at Astermore and yet have made no effort to contact me. As such, you will remedy this by joining me this afternoon.*

She groaned. Refusal was impossible, as was delaying it. Her grandmother would only be angrier if she postponed.

"Is everything all right, Lady Thea?" Mr. Vane asked as he came down the stairs. He had been nothing but polite during his stay, but something seemed to have changed between their interactions. He seemed unusually interested in her, constantly asking her to join him during activities. Riding had only been the first of many, and unlike riding, she didn't have an excuse to get out of most of it. Perhaps his family was pressuring him to marry as well. Considering Ilene's behavior, Thea wouldn't be surprised.

"Just a letter from my grandmother," she said lightly. It was a family matter and those stayed within the family. Despite him being Ilene's brother, he was not Thea's family.

The only good thing about being summoned by her grandmother was that she wouldn't be available to entertain Mr. Vane. There would be no strolls in the garden or long walks to town with him today.

She walked into the breakfast room and felt more than heard him following behind her. Every dinner, he had been seated beside her and despite Cecil's presence at breakfast, it was always as if she and Mr. Vane were eating alone.

As she prepared her plate, she wished more than ever that she could crawl back into her bed and let Bridget steal a tray from the kitchen and eat safely in the security of her room.

"HELLO, GRANDMOTHER. YOU LOOK WELL."

She leaned down to kiss her grandmother's cheek, as the older woman expected her to do. The air around her grandmother was always pungent with perfumes and it took everything in Thea not to make a face as she leaned in.

Thea straightened again and took her seat on the low, stiff Victorian couch. If it wasn't for that being the style when her grandmother moved into the Dower House, Thea would have assumed that her grandmother had picked the couch out specifically to make her guests as uncomfortable as possible so

that they didn't overstay their welcome. Meanwhile, her grandmother's chair was a higher-backed winged chair that looked
far more comfortable. Not that Thea was ever allowed to sit in
it. The cottage had been meticulously decorated for Christmas
in that over-the-top sort of way that Thea desperately hated.

Visiting the Dower House was one of her least favorite
annual traditions. Of all the social obligations she had been
able to evade, somehow this was never one. Her mother was
able to avoid coming to the Dower House because her mother
and grandmother seemed to be in a silent feud for the entirety
of Thea's life. She now wondered if it had anything to do with
her mother's pre-marital affair with Colonel Bantry. She
wouldn't be surprised if her grandmother knew and had held
that grudge for decades.

Her grandmother watched hawkishly. "Another year and
no husband."

Thea flinched and wished she could groan.

Her grandmother once told her that it would be better to
die than to be a spinster. While Thea didn't agree, death
seemed like a preferable option when faced with the constant
nagging and interrogation about her getting married. The
other person's death, obviously.

For a brief, morbid second, Thea wondered if James would
help her hide a body. While her brother said he wasn't a spy,
she wasn't entirely convinced.

Her grandmother's maid, a stiff-lipped woman who suited
her grandmother well, poured them both a cup of tea. Truth-
fully, Thea would have preferred something stronger, but she
really needed her wits about her.

"Lord Merrimere has an eligible son," her grandmother
began. "A third son, but beggars cannot be choosers, at this
rate." She shook her head. "If you had settled down earlier,
you might have been able to secure a better match."

The part about her aunt's fortune being the reason to

secure her a better husband went unsaid. Talking directly about money was terribly vulgar and her grandmother would never stoop to such levels. It was far better to allude to the fact that she thought the only reason anyone would marry Thea at this point had to be for her fortunes. Every time her grandmother spoke, she made Thea feel positively ancient at twenty-two.

It didn't help that so many her age were married. Even her cousin Stella, who was rebellious and independent, had been married when she was twenty, which only went to further prove her grandmother's point.

And she didn't dare offer up Leslie's name. That was built on hopes and wishes and daydreams when she was alone. While he had expressed interest in her, the lack of anything else left her wondering what his intentions towards her were.

"I'm sure he's lovely."

She highly doubted it. Most of the men her grandmother listed were usually horrid. Thea would endure dinner and long conversations with them when they came over or when her grandmother secured invitations to their houses for Thea and her mother, but Thea would rather be alone forever than get stuck in a loveless marriage the way Wilhelmina had.

"Excellent. I have already spoken with Ilene about it and he will be here Saturday."

It wouldn't just be the one. Ilene could never resist throwing a party. If they were having company, Ilene would want them to be balanced. A friend from school or another unmarried lady and her mother would be invited. Anyone else who lived close enough and was free would be invited if Ilene had her way. It was times like this when Thea desperately wished for a sister or two so that her family would have someone else to fuss over.

It would at least take the focus off of her.

Arnold, her grandmother's cat that Thea would have

sworn was actually a demon in disguise, watched her from his perch on the couch. She was sitting in his territory and she was sure it didn't help that she smelled like another cat. His eyes narrowed and Thea pulled her hands closer into her lap.

THEA TOOK THE FIRST CHANCE TO ESCAPE FROM THE HOUSE. Outside, the air was clear and she was thankful to finally be alone. Perhaps she shouldn't be, but she found being around her family overwhelming. The grounds were quiet. The winter air had set in and it felt beautiful.

It's only until after the new year, she reminded herself. *Then we can go home.*

She'd give anything to be able to go home. Cecil and Ilene would return in time for the Season. But Cecil spent his days in the study or in Parliament or his clubs and Ilene paid calls to the other married women and went to the different social events. It was somehow so much easier to avoid her there.

And Thea could always visit Stella at Wraughtley Place. Despite not being as close to her cousin as she was with her cousins in Scotland, Anthony and Charlie, Stella never minded if Thea invaded her house. Lord Wraughtley, Stella's husband, was a good man and Thea found him to be something of a kindred spirit. He was always more than happy to let Thea hide in the terraced house while Stella was out. In theory, this was also terribly improper, but so long as only the three of them knew, it wasn't like it would cause any trouble. Molly knew as well, but she would never betray that secret.

She breathed in the smells from the bakery and waved at the tenants she had known since she was a child.

The key still sat heavily in her pocket. Trying to follow Mercury hadn't uncovered anything. Until she knew what the key unlocked, she figured it was probably safer to keep it on her. Especially considering everything that happened at Ravenholm with the fabled treasure. If there was a treasure hidden at Astermore, she would have thought she would have heard about it before.

Taking a chance, she darted into the locksmith's shop. Bridget said the key hadn't been used in some time, but perhaps he worked on the lock it belonged to. Thea didn't know much about keys, but it was worth a shot.

"Hello?" she called out. Something metal clanged and a man let out a series of curses.

Mr. Thompson came into the shop and his eyes widened as he saw her.

"Milady, my apologies."

"Are you all right?" she asked, motioning at his hand that was bleeding and wrapped in a dirty rag.

"Just a scratch, milady." He tightened his grip on the rag. "What can I do for you?"

She fished the key out of her pocket and held it out for him. "I was wondering if you might be able to identify what this opened."

He frowned and held out his hand. "May I?"

She nodded and passed it to him. Mr. Thompson held it up to his face, studying it with an expert eye for several minutes.

"It's for a door at the manor. The late Earl had several new keys commissioned when he became lord."

"This is one of them?"

He nodded. "I made them myself when I was apprenticing. Put my mark on it I was so proud." He pointed to a tiny, almost imperceptible mark in the scrollwork.

"It's beautiful." Thea paused. "You don't happen to know what the lock it would fit would look like?"

He nodded again. "As a matter of fact, I would, milady. The late Lord Astermore asked me to make the keys to match the door handles." He hesitated a moment. "He drew the designs for the scrollwork on both."

She jolted a little at that, staring down at the key. When her father died, it had been like most of the traces of him had disappeared from the house. But the fact that he left a more permanent mark in the form of the keys and locks felt like something special.

"Did you install them as well?"

He shook his head.

For a second, she felt disappointed. But she knew who would have been there when her father had them installed and he would be more than happy to provide her with some answers.

"Thank you for your help, Mr. Thompson. And I'll call for the doctor." She held up her hand as he started to protest. "I insist. It was my fault for startling you."

"That's very kind of you, milady."

CHAPTER FOUR

THEA DIDN'T GET THE CHANCE SHE HOPED TO GO DOWNSTAIRS to ask Mr. Barton about the locks. The days were taken over with preparations for Ilene's dinner party and Thea didn't want to interrupt anyone or take them away from their work. There was enough pressure as it was, since her grandmother also planned to attend.

The house had transformed into a Christmas display overnight. Where her mother's decorations had always been warm and full of life, Ilene opted for something a little less traditional. It wasn't bad, but she missed the Christmases of her childhood.

Mr. George Rutledge, the third son of Lord Merrimere, was nothing like Thea expected. For one, he was far older than she thought.

It took her a moment to realize that Lord Merrimere was a man well into his seventies, so it made sense that his children, even the youngest, would be far older than her.

Why would her grandmother think she would have even the slightest interest in him? She supposed it didn't matter much to her grandmother. Any eligible man looking for a wife would do in her grandmother's eyes. Both of the older brothers must have already been married for her grandmother not to arrange a meeting with one of them instead.

She huffed under her breath.

"Lovely man," Mr. Vane teased. "Possibly old enough to be my father."

"I think he is older than my mother," Thea replied as quietly as she could.

Despite whatever interest Mr. Vane had in her, for some reason, he decided that she would never look at him that way. This was for the best as she valued him as her niece's uncle and godfather, but didn't want to have a romantic relationship with him and especially didn't want to make things awkward between them. They would see each other for the rest of their lives at family occasions and the last thing she wanted was for them to have tension there.

"I hope they don't expect you to have anything in common with him."

Thea glanced at her grandmother who was sitting on the other side of the room while they waited to go through for dinner. "I don't think they care."

"It's not too late. We could always run away." She looked back at him to find him smirking.

She had not worn her fanciest dress, which her mother might have commented under any other circumstances. But her mother didn't seem to like the whole scheme with Mr. Rutledge any more than Thea did.

Her mother had never forced potential suitors at her. Until recently, Thea never gave it much thought. But perhaps that was because of her mother's past. It wouldn't have made much sense for her to make her children endure the same thing that she had.

Mr. Rutledge seemed more interested in her mother than he did in Thea. Other than a very brief greeting, he had quickly introduced himself to her mother, much to her grand-mother's horror.

"Where would we run?"

"Wherever you'd like."

If Mr. Rutledge had shown the slightest bit of interest in her, she might have been tempted to take him up on that offer. As it was, he had hardly acknowledged her presence.

"Somehow, I think I'll survive."

Mr. Vane shrugged. "Your loss, my lady. I've been told I am an excellent partner in untimely escapes."

"Oh?" She smiled. "Then perhaps you should find the young lady who told you that, as she's clearly delusional enough to believe it."

He held his heart. "You wound me. How shall I ever recover?"

"I'm sure you'll figure out something."

Her grandmother's gaze turned to them and Thea's blood ran cold.

"Pretend like you're interested in our conversation. Quickly, please."

He frowned, turning his body more towards hers. "I am interested in our conversation. There's no need for me to pretend." His voice lost the teasing tone. "I enjoy spending time with you, Lady Thea. In another life, I might have loved you."

She frowned. "In another life?"

She thought... she had been so sure that he was trying to pursue something.

His expression grew somber, though he kept himself angled just enough that her grandmother wouldn't be able to see his face clearly. His voice was soft and she knew without a doubt he didn't want to be overheard.

"I was in love." He paused. "It didn't end well."

"I'm sorry."

He shook his head. "Some things are just not meant to be."

"That's…" She didn't want to say 'terribly sad', though that was how she felt. "I don't know what to say."

He lifted the corner of his lips, but there was no joy to it. "You don't need to say anything. We can't change the past."

Something about that felt so final. While whoever he loved might still be alive, it was like they were dead anyway. Thea had never really been in love before, at least nothing that would create the notes of pain that were so heavy in his voice.

"Ilene thinks that she can help me move past it." He shrugged. "Sometimes, it's easier to play along with what's expected of you rather than fight it."

She let out a breath. "I know what you mean."

All she ever did was pretend she was okay. She was tired of only ever doing what was expected of her. It was time to move past that and live for something better.

———

THEA WALKED DOWN THE STAIRS AFTER BREAKFAST. IT WASN'T hard to get into the servants' areas at Astermore, but it felt taboo now where it hadn't as a child. Perhaps it truly no longer was her home.

"My lady!" Everyone climbed to their feet immediately. Downstairs at Astermore Manor was run more strictly than Prescott House. While they would never dare disrespect her there, the atmosphere was never so stiff upon seeing her in the kitchens. She often snuck down for a late-night snack or to sit with Bridget while Bridget did her mending or played cards with Ezra, Anna, and Winnie. It was a bit more unorthodox than a house of Astermore's size.

She took a breath before she spoke. "I'm looking for Mr. Barton."

A young footman that she didn't recognize stepped forward. "I can fetch him for you, my lady."

She shook her head. "Is he down here?"

"He's in the pantry, my lady."

Thea nodded and turned before any of them could say another word.

Despite the house no longer being her home, she still knew her way around downstairs. After all, she had spent many nights downstairs as a little girl. Mr. Barton would make her hot cocoa or warm milk when she had nightmares and he had comforted her after her aunt and her father's deaths.

The door was closed, so she raised a hand to knock. The footman had followed her. She could hear his footsteps struggling to catch up with her.

"My lady," Mr. Barton greeted as he opened the door. "What can I do for you?"

It was at that point that the footman finally reached them. Mr. Barton raised his brow in response.

"Did you need something, John?"

John glanced at Thea. "No, sir."

He nodded and the young man turned and walked away.

"My lady," Mr. Barton said again.

"Do you mind if we step inside?"

"Of course." He pulled the door open the rest of the way and Thea walked in.

"I wanted to ask you something…" She trailed off as she glanced towards the door. Mr. Barton nodded and closed it.

"What is it, my lady?"

She reached into her pocket and pulled out the key for him. "I spoke with Mr. Thompson, the locksmith, and he said my father had them commissioned when he became earl. I wondered if you knew which locks were replaced."

"May I?" he asked, holding out his hand. Thea nodded and handed him the key. "Where did you find this?"

"My cat brought it back." She cringed at how that sounded. "He has a tendency to find shiny things. He escaped from my room a few times and one of the times, he brought this back."

"I see." He turned it over in his hands. "It's not exactly a secret that the late Lord Astermore and the Dowager Countess didn't see eye to eye on many things." Thea frowned. "His mother, my lady."

She blinked. To be honest, she couldn't remember many of their interactions clearly. Her grandmother always seemed so disapproving of everyone and everything that Thea hadn't paid much attention to how she treated the rest of her family.

"He changed the locks on rooms so my grandmother couldn't get in."

Mr. Barton inclined his head.

"Do you know which rooms?"

He nodded and moved to his desk. He opened one of the drawers and pulled out a book. "I made a list at the time." He hesitated. "A few of the keys went missing just shortly before your father's passing. I thought his lordship might inquire about them, but he never did and so the issue was never pursued."

Thea stared at the page that Mr. Barton opened to. The list was written in his tiny, neat little handwriting. "May I borrow this?"

He bowed his head again. "Of course, my lady."

She didn't plan to keep it forever, but for now, it would be helpful in trying to find which door the key went to.

CHAPTER FIVE

"LADY THEA," MR. VANE CALLED TO HER. THEA PAUSED ON her way to the library and he stopped in front of her. "I was wondering if we might go for a walk."

Thea took a breath, then nodded. "I would enjoy that."

Walking with Mr. Vane outside was rather pleasant. It was nice to go outside and get away from her thoughts. Ever since Mercury brought her the key, it had been all she could think of. She had tried following her cat again, but he managed to slip away every time.

If she didn't know better, she would have said her father planned for her to find the key. He had no way of knowing that Mercury would be there though or that her kitten liked collecting shiny objects.

"You're a hard person to find."

Thea glanced at him, but he didn't elaborate.

"Being back here is strange," she said when it was clear he wouldn't say anymore.

"How so?"

"It doesn't feel like the home I grew up in. I feel..."

"Feel?" he prompted.

She sighed. "I feel that I'm a constant source of disappointment when I'm here." He blinked and she continued. "It's
different for you. You're a son." She looked out at the forest as
they strolled. "My mother is so happy every time she's here.
Even if it upsets her, she sees Cecil and Ilene and is happy. I
feel out of place when I'm here."

She didn't feel that way in London. When she was there,
with Leslie and James and Wilhelmina and Molly, it felt like she
had finally found where she belonged. She missed them all
terribly and had written Wilhelmina and Molly every day, since
both of them refused to use a telephone.

James had been hesitant to talk where he thought the rest
of their family could overhear her speaking to him, but he said
he sent her Christmas gift with Bridget. Thea wished she could
be with him when he opened his present from her. She had
spent weeks sewing a Christmas stocking for him that featured
the Astermore goose prominently. She wanted to give him
something that was a tangible reminder that he was a part of
their family.

Thea had called Leslie while she had been at Astermore as
well, and it had been nice to hear his voice, but she felt like she
had been looking over her shoulder the whole time. Ilene
would have been thrilled that Thea was interested in someone,
but Cecil probably would be less thrilled. He always seemed to
have his own plans for her. It was strange to think that if she
had lived a few decades earlier, London wouldn't have been far
enough outside of Cecil's reach for the majority of the year.

The new year couldn't come fast enough.

Mr. Vane frowned, coming to a stop. For a moment, she
wondered if he was going to insist that they did everything out
of love, no matter how hurtful it felt.

"There's something I've been dying to know," he said
instead.

"Oh?"

Mr. Vane nodded seriously. "Astermore won't say and Ilene doesn't know."

Thea glanced at him. "I'm curious now. What is it?"

"Why is your family crest a goose?"

The question wasn't one she had been expecting, especially not with the way the conversation had been going. She laughed and he stared at her expectantly.

"The way my father used to tell the story, it was supposed to be a joke." Mr. Vane cocked his head. "The first earl supposedly chose it because his wife-to-be stole a goose for him."

"Did she really?"

Thea shook her head. "No one actually knows."

CHAPTER SIX

I⊤ TURNED OUT THAT IT WASN'T AS SIMPLE AS NARROWING DOWN which of the doors her father had the locks replaced on. Before he died, he had locked a number of the rooms on the second floor and it seemed that no one had bothered with them since.

Why hadn't Cecil changed the locks? It seemed silly to have a part of the floor closed with no explanation. Although, with just the three of them living in Astermore full time, they didn't really need the rooms opened. Still, Thea was curious.

It turned out the reason why Cecil never noticed the rooms were locked was because they hadn't actually been locked. Mr. Barton forgot to tell her that the doors hadn't been locked in nearly five years. If none of the doors on Mr. Barton's list were locked, the key was a bit useless to her. She thought it would lead to some grand mystery.

Instead, it lead to nothing but disappointment. She hadn't even found the door that the key matched, nor the other keys that had gone missing.

It was with that, she wandered back downstairs.

"Mr. Barton," Thea called as she saw him walking down the hall. She held out the book to him. "Thank you."

"You found which room the key went to then, my lady?"

She shook her head. "Unfortunately no." She glanced away. Outside looked chilly, but it was still bright out and it would be good to take a walk and clear her head.

"If anyone asks after me, tell them I'm taking a walk."

"Of course, my lady."

Thea walked back to her room, opened her wardrobe and took out her coat, and headed outside. The key weighed heavily in her pocket. Despite proving to be useless, she was reluctant to give it up. It was a piece of her father and she wanted to keep that close to her.

She closed her eyes and tried to picture him standing on the grounds beside her. He always went with her on walks. They would go across the bridges, heading towards the town. She loved the spot where they used to stand, where they could see the whole village from the grounds. The waters that had once been a moat when the land held a castle that was long destroyed still surrounded the property.

The house had originally been called Astermore Castle. Her great-grandfather felt it was too grand for the house, despite some of the remnants of the original castle that still stood, such as the gatehouse. The castle itself was long demolished and the house had been built in its place. But Thea had always loved the bits of the history that remained.

Her father loved them too, she remembered as she wandered closer to the gatehouse. He had taken great care to restore the gatehouse into being a usable building. The windows had been repaired.

Thea paused. It would only make sense if he had replaced the locks out there as well. The gardener, Mr. Wakefield, lived on the ground floor, but Thea remembered her father bringing her upstairs more than once. Cecil would never have bothered to go out there, since it was a servant's quarters.

She knocked on the door. There was a good chance that he

wasn't home, since it was the middle of the day, so she was surprised when he opened the door.

"My lady. This is a surprise."

"I'm sorry to drop by unexpectedly."

He shook his head. "Not at all. Won't you step in from the cold?"

"Thank you."

The gatehouse was a pleasant change after standing outside. He had a fire roaring that warmed the room.

"I have a bit of a strange question," she started. "The room upstairs… I found a key and was wondering if belonged to it."

His brow furrowed.

"I wouldn't know, my lady. I never disturbed that room."

She nodded. "Do you mind if I check?"

He shook his head. "Not at all."

The stairs were situated on the outside wall of the gate-house. She could have easily walked into the building without alerting Mr. Wakefield to her presence as she and her father had done so many times when she was younger. But after not visiting this room in years, it felt rude to just walk into his home when he hadn't been used to being disturbed.

Thea climbed up the stairs and turned at the first floor. Sure enough, the door was locked. It was strange to think that the last person who might have been in there had been her father. She pulled the key from her pocket and slipped it into the door. It opened without any issue.

The door creaked open, the way a door that hadn't been used in far too long did. The hinges seemed to fight her a bit and it took some effort as she pushed it open. The room was covered in a thick layer of dust. Everything in it had clearly not been moved or touched in years. Despite the dust, Thea closed the door behind her. She wanted a chance to look around without Mr. Wakefield walking in.

The room hadn't warmed at all from the fire roaring downstairs. The stone walls didn't help to insulate from the chill in the air. The lack of anything warm in the room, such as drapes or rugs, also didn't help. Thea pulled her coat tighter. It would be worth it to wear heavier clothes when she came back.

The desk her father put out here was still there though. The ceiling was solid and she didn't see any leaks or cracks. She would have to check the floor above it. The gatehouse's second floor was smaller and back when it was a functional gatehouse, had functioned as the place where they watched for trouble.

When she was very young, she used to climb up to the second floor and peer through the arrowslits that lined the outside and imagine she was a princess trapped in a tower waiting for the armies to come for her. There was a whole battle scene she made up in her head, but she doubted that if she wrote it, anyone would actually want to read it.

The desk was exactly as her father left it that day. She sat down in the chair and reached for the drawers. They wobbled but otherwise didn't budge. Her father had left a spare key hidden in the room for the drawers, since he was always losing his key for it. Was it in the same spot he last left it?

She felt under the desk, but it was clear he had moved it. That spot had been far too obvious. Thea glanced around the room. If she had been him, where would he have hidden it?

Under the rug was another far too obvious spot.

The room didn't have any paintings or books. He never put in bookshelves and Thea had a feeling the desk had actually been there longer than her father had been alive and he had only replaced the lock so that he was the only one able to get in.

She glanced at the empty fireplace. Nothing had burned in the fireplace in years. It would be the perfect spot to hide things. And he had been to Ravenholm Castle more than once, since his sister Diana married Malcolm McNeil, the Earl of

Ravenholm. It would make sense that he had heard stories about the hidden passages there.

It wasn't like Astermore lacked hidden passages, but the new house was only built in the late 1600s. It hadn't needed the many hidden priest holes that other homes needed, since it had been built after the Prescotts turned Anglican, like the rest of England. She was sure that the castle probably would have had more, but all that remained of it were the ruins by the deer park and the gatehouse.

She looked at the fireplace, analyzing it carefully. Every stone was firmly in place. Thea wasn't sure what made her crouch down and try to move the stones in the walls inside the fireplace anyway. Perhaps it was just remembering her experiences at Ravenholm, but it paid off. One of the stones came loose.

Thea hesitated. She didn't really want to put her hand inside a dark hole in the wall with no idea of what was inside. Without laying flat on the floor, she wouldn't be able to to get low enough to see inside and she definitely didn't want to have to explain how she had gotten so filthy if she encountered anyone before she could change clothes. Her gloves were thick enough to provide protection, she supposed as she stuck her hand into the hole. It didn't stop her from squeezing her eyes shut and turning her head away.

Her fingers met something in there. It was solid and she grabbed at it until it slipped forward enough for her to grip it properly. The key was as filthy as the room, caked with dirt and grime and discolored from age and air. She couldn't believe her father hid the key inside the wall. What was in the desk that he had been worried that someone might find?

She brushed her hands together, watching as the dirt floated to the floor, then brushed her clothes off with her cleaner hand. At least her clothes were a reasonably dark green and someone would have to be looking closely in order to see how dirty she had gotten. Bridget would be annoyed that she spoiled her clothes though. Perhaps even more annoyed that Thea left her behind while she looked out here. But she couldn't bear the idea of someone else in the place that had just been her and her father's secret.

Thea sat down at the desk again and slipped the key into the desk lock. Despite years of disuse, it didn't fight her too badly. The drawer stuck a bit, but she was finally able to force it open.

The missing keyring of keys sat in the top of the drawer. What was underneath them took her breath away. She pulled the keyring out and set it on the desk before she took a closer look.

"Dorothea Seton Dead on a Fatal Ride," she read under her breath. She pushed that paper aside. The next was the death certificate. A coroner's report. Another newspaper with a similar title and account.

What was her father doing with this? Why was he looking into her aunt's death before he died?

Thea stared at the papers in the drawer for several minutes. He had been looking into Thea's aunt, her mother's sister's death. The aunt that Thea had been with when she died. What had he found?

Her father had been the one to introduce her to mysteries and detective stories. He used to read them to her when she was a little girl. She never realized that she might have gotten her desire to investigate from him.

She pushed the drawer shut and removed the key from the drawers. If no one had come up there in years, it was probably safe enough to leave it there for right now. She would hide the key to the drawer in this room. Not behind the stone where she found it, as the dust had been moved and it would be too obvious. There was a small crevice she used to tuck things between under the window as a girl. If someone somehow stumbled upon the room and got inside, they wouldn't know to look there. She checked that she would still be able to remove it before she moved back to the desk and placed the keyring in her pocket.

Mr. Barton would appreciate that they had been found, but she wouldn't have someone stumbling upon this before she could study it better.

Why hadn't her father hidden any of it better? She supposed it had been hidden well, considering no one ever come across it in five years, not until Thea went actively looking for the lock that fit the key. And she wouldn't have done that if Mercury hadn't found the key in the first place. Had her father hidden the key to the gatehouse inside Astermore or merely dropped it where no one had found it for years?

Brushing herself off one last time, Thea headed back to the door and locked it once more. She checked the handle to make sure it latched firmly before she glanced down the stairs. Mr. Wakefield was nowhere in sight, so she opened her blouse slightly and slipped the key beneath her corset. The weight felt odd, but it was better that no one saw her with it again and asked any questions. She would give Bridget the keys with a story about how Mercury found them and tell her to return them to Mr. Barton. There would be fewer questions that way. At least until she could figure out what had happened.

When she was back in her room, she would hide the key to the door better until she could visit the room again. With that decided, she turned and walked carefully back down the stairs.

Mr. Wakefield was eating his meal. He stood as he saw her. "Would you like some tea, my lady? Or perhaps something to eat?"

She shook her head. "No, thank you. I was just wondering… do you happen to remember when my father last came here?"

Mr. Wakefield blinked. "I believe it was the day he passed, my lady. He came early that morning before I started work."

She felt faint, her head spinning at the thought. What exactly was in those papers and why had her father kept them away from the main house? Had he discovered something more about her aunt's death?

"My lady," Mr. Wakefield said as he took her arm. Until that moment, she didn't realize how unsteady she had grown. He guided her to a chair and she sat down. The room stopped spinning quite as much. "Perhaps I should see you back to the main house."

She shook her head.

"I'm all right. Really."

"You look like you've had a shock."

She let out a shuddering breath. "I... I was just taken off guard. I didn't realize that it would look exactly as he left it. Would it be too much to ask that you don't let anyone go upstairs?"

He frowned. "My lady, no one but you and his lordship... your father... ever comes—came out here."

She nodded. "It's just my father and I did a lot up there together... he used to tell me stories when we went up there and look at the stars... and I'd like to keep his memory alive a bit longer." She hoped that didn't sound completely unreasonable. It was far better than 'my father left papers up there and I think he may have been investigating my aunt's death. She forced a smile on her face. "I hate to intrude on you any longer today, but I'll be back in a few days."

Mr. Wakefield smiled and nodded. "Of course, my lady. You're welcome anytime."

With that, Thea stood up again. She smiled at him, even though it was hard to smile with how shaken she felt. Mr. Wakefield walked her to the door. The cold air outside hit her face and she fought the urge to stay in the gardener's warm home. She wouldn't intrude any longer today, lest she roused suspicion.

She needed a basket or something to hide the papers in. If she put Mercury in the basket with many blankets, perhaps that wouldn't rouse too much suspicion. It wouldn't be suspicious for her to bring her kitten with her. She wasn't sure who she could trust with this.

Perhaps she would look for some sort of small gift for Mr. Wakefield as well, such as a tin of tea. It would certainly give her an excuse to visit so her family wasn't suspicious of why she was visiting the gardener.

A figure crossed the grounds in the distance. He walked past the house and headed towards her. Thea frowned, trying to get a better look at them. Who would be looking for her on the grounds?

"Leslie," she gasped. She tried to ignore the way her cheeks heated. It was just from the wind. She pulled her coat tighter as she stepped closer to him. "What are you doing here?"

"I hope you don't mind me dropping by unannounced. I was heading home for the holidays and when the train stopped, I just thought…"

She smiled. "I don't mind at all. Will you be staying for dinner?"

As much as she'd like him to stay, she prayed that he'd say no. The last thing she wanted was Ilene to scare him away by asking if they would be getting married.

"I wouldn't want to intrude." He set his case on the bench and opened it. "I wanted to bring you your present."

Thea blinked. "I'm sorry. I actually sent your gift on to Hollindale Abbey."

She wished she had known he was coming. She wished she could see his face when he opened her gift, a set of silk handkerchiefs that she had embroidered with his initials and family crest. It was a bit improper to be sending a man who wasn't openly courting her a Christmas gift. They weren't engaged and didn't actually have an understanding, so she had sent it under James' name and hoped that her brother would understand if there was any confusion. She signed the inside card with her name, but figured Leslie's family might have questions if she sent it under her own.

He shook his head. "That's quite all right."

The box was small and bright blue, wrapped with a beautifully tied ribbon. He seemed almost nervous as he handed it to her and his eyes seemed to focus more on her cheek than actually meet her eyes.

Thea untied the bow and opened the small box, pushing aside the wrapping to reveal the most beautiful comb she could remember seeing. Carved tortoise shell with dozens of tiny diamonds along the top, this was not the kind of gift one gave a casual acquaintance.

The gift was permanent. Lasting. Her cheeks felt hot at the thought. Any gift she received from other men not related to her was usually something small and perishable and usually gone or dead by the end of the year, such as fruits or candies or flowers. This was a declaration of something much more that that.

"It's beautiful."

She shouldn't accept it. What did it say about her if she accepted it? A comb like this was an heirloom, something one would pass down to their children. One might wear it on their wedding day, though she would wear her family's tiara if… when she got married.

Thea stared at it a second longer before she looked up. "Thank you."

Relief seemed to flood him and his shoulders relaxed.

"I should probably go," he said softly and she wondered if he had walked from the station. "May I call on you back in London?"

"I'd love that."

Leslie leaned in and pressed his lips against the corner of her mouth. Before she could think too much about what she was doing, Thea turned her head. Her free hand gripped his collar and pulled him closer. The world might have stopped at that moment and she wouldn't have cared.

"Happy Christmas, Thea," he whispered, his breath warm against her lips.

"Happy Christmas."

To be continued…

Thank you for reading A Lady Thea Mystery.
Thea, Mercury, and her friends will return in
future adventures.

- Jessica

Sign up for my newsletter to be notified about the continuation of this mystery and future adventures set in the world of Lady Thea.

CHARACTERS

Lady Theodora Prescott-Pryce – Thea lives with her widowed mother in London.

Mercury - Thea's mischievous black kitten.

Vivien Astermore - The Dowager Lady Astermore - mother of Thea and the current Earl of Astermore.

Cecil - The Earl of Astermore - Thea's younger brother and Ilene's husband.

Ilene - The Countess of Astermore - Cecil's wife, Thea's sister-in-law, and Colin's sister. Mother to Thea's niece, Zoe.

The Dowager Countess Prudentia Prescott-Pryce - Thea and Cecil's paternal grandmother.

Colin Vane - Ilene's brother and Zoe's godfather.

Detective Inspector Leslie Thayne a.k.a. the Honorable Edward Leslie Thayne – the younger son of a Scottish Baron and works in the Criminal Investigation Department of Scotland Yard.

Mr. Barton - butler at Astermore Manor.

Bridget Semple - Thea's new lady's maid who traveled with her from Scotland.

ALSO SET IN THEA'S WORLD:

ABOUT THE AUTHOR

Named for the famous fictional mystery writer Jessica Fletcher, Jessica Baker picked up a pen when she was in elementary school and never set it down.

Jessica lives in sunny Central Florida and is a member of the National Sisters in Crime. When she's not writing, she works at a university and freelances as a camera assistant in film which provides plenty of inspiration for her stories.

To learn more about Jessica and her books, visit her at www.jessicabakerauthor.com and for the latest information, subscribe to her newsletters.

Printed in Great Britain
by Amazon

17436421R00036